BBC Tweenies™

Never be Scared of a Dragon

One day, Milo dressed up as a brave knight.
"Don't worry, Judy," he said. "Sir Milo will
rescue you from the scary dragon!"

"Oh, thank you, Milo! " she laughed.
Then Jake asked, "What is a dragon, exactly?"
"Perhaps we should ask Sir Milo," replied Judy. "He's always fighting them. Milo?"

Milo stopped. He wasn't absolutely sure.

"Well ... er ... they're very big and scary and ... er ... knights fight them."

"They have wings and breathe fire," said Bella.

Judy showed them a drawing of a dragon in a book. "Yes, Bella's right. Look, they're like huge lizards with scaly skin, little wings and long pointed tails, and they do breathe fire."

"Judy, could we do our own picture of a dragon?" asked Fizz.

"That's a splendid idea," agreed Judy. The others cheered, but Milo wasn't interested in making a picture.

"Brave Sir Milo doesn't waste his time drawing dragons. He's ready to fight the real thing!" "Well, do you mind doing it outside?" asked Judy. "And put your scarf on. You've only just got over your cold, remember."

Outside, Milo ran round the climbing frame,
swishing his sword and stabbing the air.
Then, suddenly...

Milo spun round and there, in front of his very eyes, was a dragon. A green scaly dragon.

"Atchhoo!" it sneezed again. Milo ran to hide under the climbing frame.

Crouched in his hiding place,
Milo heard the dragon
sneeze four more times.
He began to feel sorry for it.
The dragon was only little,
and seemed to have a
terrible cold.

Then, to Milo's amazement, the dragon waved and spoke to him.

"Hello. I wonder if you could help me?"

Milo edged forward, pointing his sword out in front of him. "H...h...hello!" he stuttered.

The dragon jumped back.

"Oh, sorry," said Milo, "It's OK. I won't hurt you."

The dragon sneezed again.

"You're a dragon, aren't you?" asked Milo.

"Sort of," the dragon replied sadly.

"Well, you've got scaly skin and wings and a pointy tail."

"But there's one very important thing missing," said the dragon. "I can't breathe fire. Look!"

It huffed and puffed, but nothing happened. "Oh dear," said Milo. "Is that because you've got a cold?"

"Yes," sniffed the dragon. Milo thought it was going to cry. What could he do to help?

"I know!" thought Milo. "When I had a cold, everyone told me to wrap up warm."

Milo took a small step closer to the dragon and wound his scarf round its neck. "How's that?"

"Lovely and cosy. I feel much warmer already."

But then, "Milo!"

"I have to go in," Milo said.

"Of course," said the dragon. "Thank you so much. You've been a most kind, brave knight."

"As you're feeling warmer, how about trying to breathe some fire before I go?" asked Milo.

The dragon cleared its throat, took a deep breath and blew.

A small orange flame appeared from its mouth.

"It's working!" cried the dragon. "Can I keep your scarf until I feel quite better?"

"No problem," said Milo. "Do you know, I was scared of you at first!"

"Never be scared of a dragon.
Especially one with a cold! See you soon!"
"Bye!" called Milo and he rushed inside.

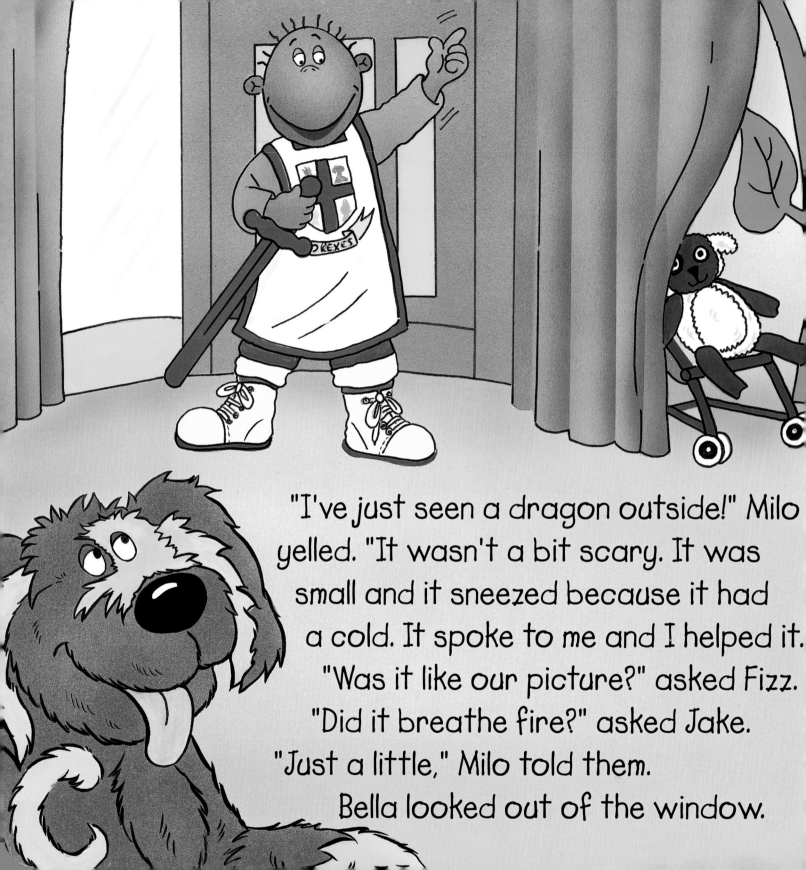

"I've just seen a dragon outside!" Milo yelled. "It wasn't a bit scary. It was small and it sneezed because it had a cold. It spoke to me and I helped it.

"Was it like our picture?" asked Fizz.

"Did it breathe fire?" asked Jake.

"Just a little," Milo told them.

Bella looked out of the window.

"I can't see a dragon. Just your scarf on the ground."
"It must be feeling better now, so it's gone home," said Milo.

Milo went ouside to pick up his scarf.
When he came back, he looked at
the dragon picture.
   "There's one thing missing," he said.
He'd started to draw a scarf
on the dragon's neck
when...

It was Doodles!

"Here you are, mate," said Milo. "Brave Sir Milo to the rescue again!" And he wrapped the warm scarf round Doodles's furry neck.

"Thank you!" sniffed Doodles.

THE END